Hansel and Gretel

First published in 2005 by
Franklin Watts
96 Leonard Street
London
EC2A 4XD

Franklin Watts Australia
45–51 Huntley Street
Alexandria
NSW 2015

Text © Penny Dolan 2005
Illustration © Graham Philpot 2005

A CIP catalogue record for this book is available
from the British Library.

ISBN 0 7496 6150 X (hbk)
ISBN 0 7496 6162 3 (pbk)

Series Editor: Jackie Hamley
Series Advisor: Dr Barrie Wade
Series Designer: Peter Scoulding

Printed in China

Hansel and Gretel

Retold by Penny Dolan

Illustrated by Graham Philpot

W
FRANKLIN WATTS
LONDON•SYDNEY

Hansel and Gretel lived
near a dark forest.

One day, they got lost
deep among the trees.

Soon, Hansel and Gretel
were very hungry.

Then they saw a pretty cottage, made of sweets and gingerbread.

Hansel and Gretel nibbled
away like hungry mice.

Suddenly, the door opened. "Come inside, dear children," an old woman smiled sweetly.

11

Then she locked the door.

She was a wicked witch!

"How dare you eat my

cottage?" she screeched.

"Now, I will eat you, boy! And you, lazy girl, can get to work!"

The witch locked Hansel
in a chicken cage.
"You are too skinny to
eat now," she snarled,
"but I will fatten you up!"

Each day, the witch fed
Hansel lots of sweets and
gingerbread.

And each day, she felt
Hansel's finger to see if he
was fat enough to eat.

But Hansel knew the witch
couldn't see well, so he held
out a chicken bone instead.

"Still too thin!" grumbled the witch.

Soon the witch grew tired of waiting. "I shall eat you tomorrow!" she screeched.

The next morning, the witch decided to eat both children.

She said to Gretel craftily:
"Climb into the oven to
see if it's hot enough."

"I don't know how," said
clever Gretel. "Show me."

"Stupid girl! Like this!"
snarled the witch. The
witch bent right over ...

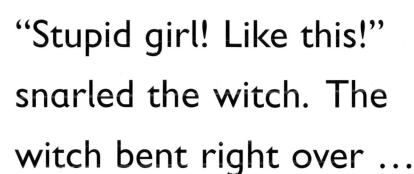

… and Gretel pushed her inside the oven and slammed the door.

Gretel let Hansel out of
the cage.

They took the witch's
stolen treasure.

Then Hansel and Gretel found their way out of the dark forest, and lived happily ever after.

31

Leapfrog has been specially designed to fit the requirements of the National Literacy Strategy. It offers real books for beginning readers by top authors and illustrators.

There are 31 Leapfrog stories to choose from:

The Bossy Cockerel
Written by Margaret Nash,
illustrated by Elisabeth Moseng

Bill's Baggy Trousers
Written by Susan Gates,
illustrated by Anni Axworthy

Mr Spotty's Potty
Written by Hilary Robinson,
illustrated by Peter Utton

Little Joe's Big Race
Written by Andy Blackford,
illustrated by Tim Archbold

The Little Star
Written by Deborah Nash,
illustrated by Richard Morgan

The Cheeky Monkey
Written by Anne Cassidy,
illustrated by Lisa Smith

Selfish Sophie
Written by Damian Kelleher,
illustrated by Georgie Birkett

Recycled!
Written by Jillian Powell,
illustrated by Amanda Wood

Felix on the Move
Written by Maeve Friel,
illustrated by Beccy Blake

Pippa and Poppa
Written by Anne Cassidy,
illustrated by Philip Norman

Jack's Party
Written by Ann Bryant,
illustrated by Claire Henley

The Best Snowman
Written by Margaret Nash,
illustrated by Jörg Saupe

Eight Enormous Elephants
Written by Penny Dolan,
illustrated by Leo Broadley

Mary and the Fairy
Written by Penny Dolan,
illustrated by Deborah Allwright

The Crying Princess
Written by Anne Cassidy,
illustrated by Colin Paine

Jasper and Jess
Written by Anne Cassidy,
illustrated by François Hall

The Lazy Scarecrow
Written by Jillian Powell,
illustrated by Jayne Coughlin

The Naughty Puppy
Written by Jillian Powell,
illustrated by Summer Durantz

Freddie's Fears
Written by Hilary Robinson,
illustrated by Ross Collins

Cinderella
Written by Barrie Wade,
illustrated by Julie Monks

The Three Little Pigs
Written by Maggie Moore,
illustrated by Rob Hefferan

Jack and the Beanstalk
Written by Maggie Moore,
illustrated by Steve Cox

The Three Billy Goats Gruff
Written by Barrie Wade,
illustrated by Nicola Evans

Goldilocks and the Three Bears
Written by Barrie Wade,
illustrated by Kristina Stephenson

Little Red Riding Hood
Written by Maggie Moore,
illustrated by Paula Knight

Rapunzel
Written by Hilary Robinson,
illustrated by Martin Impey

Snow White
Written by Anne Cassidy,
illustrated by Melanie Sharp

The Emperor's New Clothes
Written by Karen Wallace,
illustrated by François Hall

The Pied Piper of Hamelin
Written by Anne Adeney,
illustrated by Jan Lewis

Hansel and Gretel
Written by Penny Dolan,
illustrated by Graham Philpot

The Sleeping Beauty
Written by Margaret Nash,
illustrated by Barbara Vagnozzi